D0598202

To Allen, the best Lefty Lou ever. —L. G.

For my mum, who taught me never to wait for a prince
and always to pursue my passions. —L. V.

STERLING CHILDREN'S BOOKS
New York

An Imprint of Sterling Publishing Co., Inc.
1166 Avenue of the Americas
New York, NY 10036

STERLING CHILDREN'S BOOKS and the distinctive Sterling Children's Books logo
are registered trademarks of Sterling Publishing Co., Inc.

Text © 2017 by Leslie Gorin
Illustrations © 2017 by Lesley Vamos

All rights reserved. No part of this publication may be reproduced, stored in a retrieval system,
or transmitted in any form or by any means (including electronic, mechanical, photocopying, recording,
or otherwise) without prior written permission from the publisher.

ISBN 978-1-4549-1817-2

Library of Congress Cataloging-in-Publication Data

Names: Gorin, Leslie, author. | Vamos, Lesley, illustrator.
Title: Elly and the smelly sneaker : a riches to rags story / Leslie Gorin ;
    illustrated by Lesley Vamos.
Description: New York : Sterling Children's Books, [2017] | Summary: In this
    twist on "Cinderella," Lefty Lou, designated fairy godfather pinch-hitting
    for the fairy godmother, fulfills a proper young lady's greatest wish--to
    play on a baseball team.
Identifiers: LCCN 2016014361 | ISBN 9781454918172 (hc-lpc with jacket picture
    book)
Subjects: | CYAC: Baseball—Fiction. | Magic—Fiction.
Classification: LCC PZ7.1.G657 El 2017 | DDC [E]—dc23 LC record available at
    https://lccn.loc.gov/2016014361

Distributed in Canada by Sterling Publishing Co., Inc.
c/o Canadian Manda Group, 664 Annette Street
Toronto, Ontario, Canada M6S 2C8
Distributed in the United Kingdom by GMC Distribution Services
Castle Place, 166 High Street, Lewes, East Sussex, England BN7 1XU
Distributed in Australia by NewSouth Books
45 Beach Street, Coogee, NSW 2034, Australia

For information about custom editions, special sales, and premium and corporate purchases,
please contact Sterling Special Sales at 800-805-5489 or specialsales@sterlingpublishing.com.

Manufactured in China

Lot #:
2 4 6 8 10 9 7 5 3 1
01/17

www.sterlingpublishing.com

Design by Andrea Miller and Heather Kelly
The artwork was created digitally.

ELLY and the SMELLY SNEAKER

A Riches to Rags Story

by Leslie Gorin

illustrated by Lesley Vamos

STERLING CHILDREN'S BOOKS
New York

JACKSON COUNTY LIBRARY, MEDFORD, OR
DEC   2018

Elly led a charmed life.

Her stepmother treated her like a princess.

Her stepsisters showered her with bonbons and feathered hats.

Maids scrubbed the house till it shone, making sure Elly never had a single cinder under her manicured nails.

9:00–10:15 Curtsy class

10:15–11:30 Advanced tea stirring

11:30–12:15 Handshakes for the hoity-toity

12:15–1:00 Dress for lunch

1:00–2:30 Lunch

2:30–3:15 Undress after lunch

3:15–4:15 Posture practice

4:15–5:30 Sitting down for the uppity

5:30–6:30 Dress for boring banquet

6:30–8:00 Boring banquet

8:00–9:00 Undress after boring banquet

9:01 Bedtime

But to Elly, life was a royal pain.

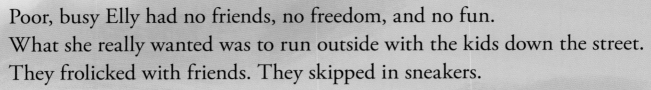

Poor, busy Elly had no friends, no freedom, and no fun.
What she really wanted was to run outside with the kids down the street.
They frolicked with friends. They skipped in sneakers.

And best of all, they played baseball.

The more Elly saw them play,
the more she longed to join them.
Sometimes, late at night, she sneaked
outside to practice on her own.

Back in bed, she dreamed of
opening days and double plays
and being on their team.

One day, a letter arrived.

"The king has issued an open invitation to the palace this morning!" said Elly's stepmother.

"Only one guest per household. Elly, your stepsisters and I insist that you go. This will be your time to shine. Ta-ta!"

Elly trudged outside, sank onto the stoop, and wept. "I'm sick of fondues and froufrous!" she wailed. "I just want to play ball!"

"Dry your eyes, kid," said a gruff voice.

Elly looked up, startled. "Who are you?" she asked.

"Lefty Lou, designated fairy godfather. I'm pinch-hitting for your fairy godmother. She's gone bungee jumping."

Elly stared in amazement.

"So you wanna play ball," said Lefty, twirling his bat.
"Well, you'll never get to first base in *that* getup."

"Bibbity,

bobbity,

BLECH!"

FOOP!

Elly's finery turned into a dusty baseball uniform, and her glass slippers became a pair of smelly sneakers.

"Just what I always wanted!" cried Elly. "Thank you!"

"Ah, fuggedaboutit!" said Lefty. "Just make sure you're back by noon. That's when the magic wears off and your threads change back to fancy duds. Now go on, get outta here! And knock one out of the park for me."

At the ballpark, the smell of hot dogs, popcorn, and excitement crackled through the air. Elly took a deep breath, then jumped right in and had a field day.

Her practice paid off as she fired off fastballs,
dove for fly balls, and hammered homers.
Pitches zipped. Bats thwacked. Fielders soared
and fans roared as Elly raced around the bases.
She had never felt so alive.

Even Elly's stepfamily stopped by. "Who *is* that?" they asked, and marveled at the dazzling new star. Elly amazed her teammates, too, and they cheered her every play. Soon the team captain, Vince, wouldn't let anyone pitch except Elly.

Elly loved the game so much, she lost track of time. During the seventh inning stretch . . .

. . . Elly jumped up and sprinted off the field.
"Gotta go!" she yelled. "Touch base later!"

"Come back!" Vince begged.
"You can't leave now—the
game is tied!"

Vince raced after her. Elly got away, but not before one of her sneakers got stuck on the mound.

As soon as she got home . . .

FOOP!

The next day, Vince went searching for Elly.
"Anyone who can wear this smelly sneaker will be
my co-captain!" he announced.

When he reached Elly's house, her stepmother answered the door.
"P. U." she said. "Get that thing away from me!"

"We wouldn't be caught dead in that!" said her stepsisters.

"I'll try it on," said Elly.

"And ruin your pedicure?" Her stepmother gasped.

But Elly stepped up to the plate and straight into the shoe. It fit perfectly, right off the bat.

As her family stood speechless, Elly pulled the matching sneaker from her purse and put it on, too.

Then Vince pulled something else from his bag. "This is yours, too, Elly," he said. "We would never have won without you."

"You won a *trophy*?" said her stepsisters.

"Playing *baseball*?" said her stepmother.

Elly nodded.

Her stepsisters gulped. Her stepmother shook her head.

Finally, in a firm voice, her stepmother said, "Elly, I'm shocked! I never dreamed you'd sneak behind my back . . .

" . . . and make me the proudest mom in the kingdom!"
Before Elly could answer, her stepsisters chimed in.

"Don't worry, Elly! You can still wear gloves . . ."

" . . . and have a coach . . ."

" . . . and you get to play on diamonds!"

Elly grinned a grin as big as a grand slam homer. "Aw, thanks!" she said, and gave everyone a major league hug.

From then on, Elly frolicked with
friends, skipped in sneakers . . .

. . . and, best of all, she and her charming Vince had a ball.

9:00–10:00	Curveball class
10:00–11:00	Advanced seed spitting
11:00–12:00	Sit-ups for the down-to-earth
12:00–1:00	Lunch (served from home plate)
1:00–2:00	Pitching for paupers
2:00–3:00	Squats for tots
3:00–4:00	Bunts for runts
4:00–5:00	Dugout benches for the unpretentious
5:00–6:00	Supper on the fly
6:00–7:00	Free time
7:00–9:00	Family time
9:01	Bedtime

The end

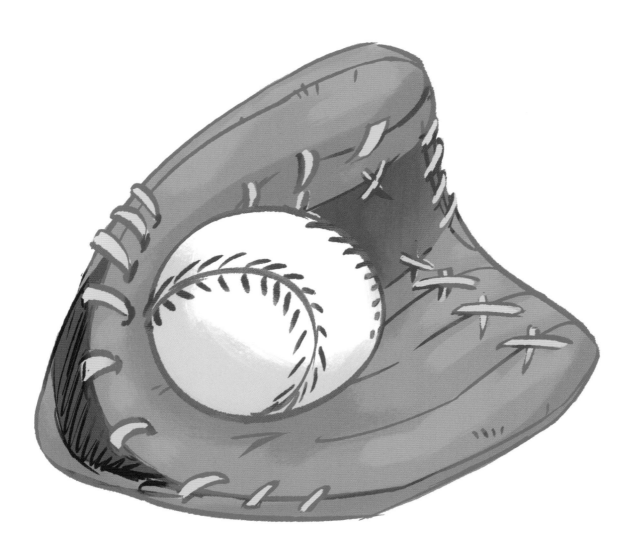

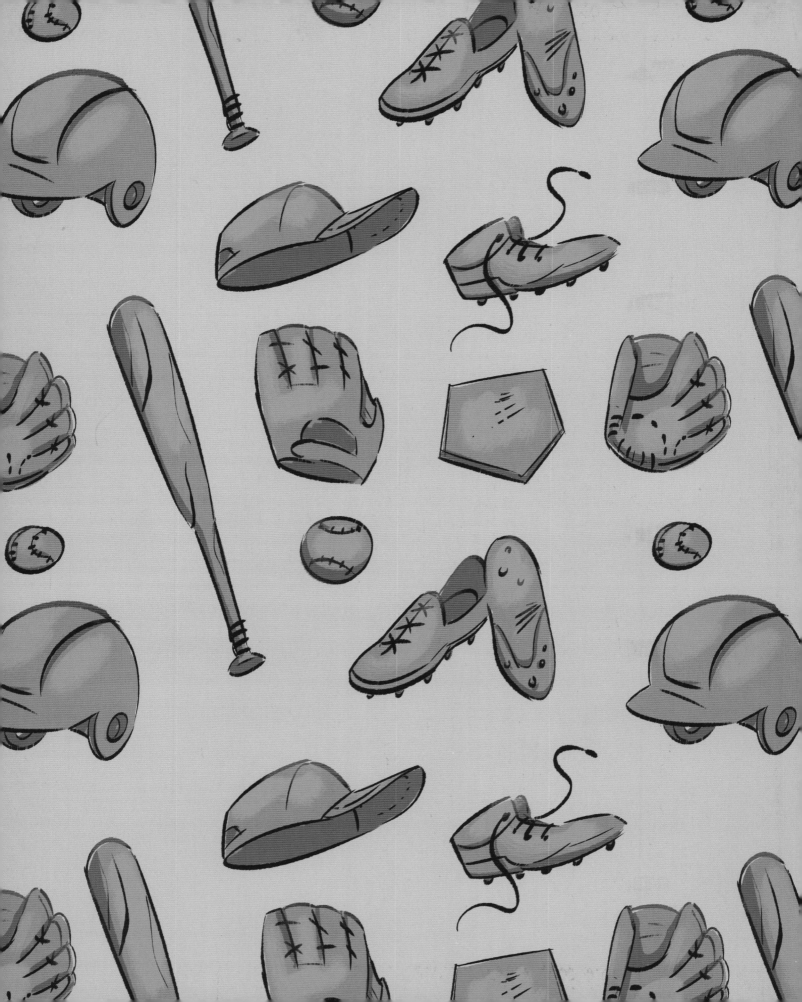